For Chauni Haslet,
who asked the question
—G. S.

For my mother and father
—D. Z.

Published in the United States in 2004 by Handprint Books
413 Sixth Avenue
Brooklyn, New York 11215
www.handprintbooks.com

First Edition
Printed in China
ISBN: 1-59354-041-8
2 4 6 8 10 9 7 5 3 1

Wise Acres

By **George Shannon**

Illustrations by **Deborah Zemke**

Handprint Books ✋ Brooklyn, New York

Help!

LIFE at Wise Acres was simply the best. Plenty of food. Long naps. The gentle care of Farmer Bill. Stories, friends, songs, and dance.

As Janet started her morning jog, the sky was blue and the breeze was sweet. Even sweeter were the sounds she heard as she neared the pond—the lush tones of Ted's banjo and Pearl's tambourine. Janet used their rehearsals to inspire a quicker pace. But a piercing "YIKES!" stopped Janet in her tracks.

When she reached the pond, Ted and Pearl
were frantically searching the water with sticks.
"Help!" cried Pearl. "I accidentally tossed my
tambourine as I gave it a big shake. It's sinking
in the pond. We can't even see it to fish it out."

Janet couldn't believe her luck. A chance to show off
her new dives *and* do a good deed!

"Never fear," called Janet. "I've been learning new dives.
I'll have your tambourine back in a flash."

Janet ran to the dock and called out the name of her
favorite dive, "Ham-smacker with a Twist!"

She had no style, but she had a lot of splash. Ted turned away quickly to keep his banjo dry. But before Pearl could think to take cover, she was dripping wet. Janet paddled to the surface with empty hooves. She jumped out of the water and charged the dock again.

"Double Pork-Chop Plop!" she called as she sailed through the air.

Her splash was twice as big. But still no tambourine.

"The water's so muddy," said Janet as she huffed and puffed her way to the dock. "I'll have to try again."

Ted and Pearl rushed to hide behind a willow, but not soon enough. Janet's third dive—a "Bacon Buster"—soaked them to the skin. And still no tambourine.

Janet stormed the dock again. But halfway to the edge, she screamed out, "Aiiiieeeee!" and fell with a bounce.

"My hoof!" she cried as she rolled down the dock. "A stone in my hoof!"

She hit the water with a plop, yelling, "Help, help, help!"

Pearl pulled her from the pond. Then Ted pulled out the stone.

Janet lay limp and dripping till she caught her breath.

"It was awful," Janet choked and began to cry. "I thought I nearly died! Please don't leave me. You've got to keep me safe."

Ted and Pearl gently held Janet's hooves till her sobbing stopped.

"Don't worry. When I'm well again in a week or two, I'll find your tambourine," Janet promised.

Sadly, Pearl looked at the pond. Her deep sigh ended
in a gasp of surprise. With no dives or poking sticks, the
water was still and clear again! Her tambourine was at
the bottom of the pond just a yard from the bank.

Pearl grabbed a fishing rod and quickly reeled in
her tambourine. Then she laid it in
the sun to dry and tighten up.

"Janet," said Pearl, "you're the greatest. You saved the day."

Ted agreed as he massaged her injured hoof. "You're always steady as a rock and twice as smart!"

"It was nothing." Janet blushed. "I'm just glad that I could help."

Mail Call

VERN looked at the mailbox. Stared at the clouds. Looked at the mailbox. Then sadly stared down the country road.

"BAAaaa," he sighed. "If I were getting any letters, they'd be here by now."

Vern walked to the barn as Hannah shook her head.
Vannah sighed. "It's been this way for five hundred days."
"Poor Vern," said Debbie. "If *only* one of us knew
the alphabet. We could send him different letters every
day of the week."

"But we don't," said Blanche. She joined Hannah, Vannah, and Savannah with a "tsk tsk tsk" as they shook their heads.

Doug grabbed his forehead and groaned a cluck. "Are you *trying* to be stupid? You don't *have* to do the writing. You can find nice letters all over the farm."

"You're a genius!" Debbie squealed. "Let's get to work. Doug will lead the way."

They swarmed through the yard like locusts after corn. They picked letters off sacks, pecked letters off a box, and pulled three labels loose. And they even took the wrapper off a loaf of bread.

"There!" said Debbie as she flipped the mailbox shut. "Vern is going to faint when he sees all the letters he got today."

"Yoo-hoo, Vern!" sang Blanche. "Have you checked the mailbox yet?"

"Why bother?" Vern sighed. But he looked anyway.

"Baaaa." He groaned as he pulled out a *T* and a *B* and *E, D, O.* "Whose idea of a joke is this? Anybody with a brain knows mailbox letters are white envelopes with *news* inside."

"Oops," whispered Hannah, Vannah, and Savannah as they tiptoed away.

"I *see*," said Debbie as she gave Blanche a wink.

The next morning, Debbie asked Doug if she could have some empty pages from his old sketchbook. But instead of drawing, she began to fold. Even then, it took all morning before she got things right. A little flour and water for a homemade paste, and Debbie had a fine white envelope.

"Oh, Vern," called Debbie when they'd finished lunch. "Have you checked to see if you got any letters today?"

"Why bother?"

Vern even refused to go *near* the mailbox. But Debbie pestered till Vern couldn't take it anymore. "Oh, all right!" grumbled Vern.

"BaaaAH!" Vern's bleat erupted with glee as he found a white envelope waiting inside.

"Stella! Look! I got a letter. Doug and Debbie, look! I did. I did! Hannah, Vannah, and Savannah! Pearl and Janet! Ted and Bob and Ray!"

Everyone came running as he opened it and cheered.

"Good news!" Vern waved the empty envelope so all could see.

"But there's nothing inside," said Doug as he rolled his eyes. "And even if there was, you don't know how to read."

Vern laughed and shook his head. "You don't *need* to know reading for news like this."

"Of course!" said Debbie as she grinned at Doug. "No news is *good* news, as *everyone* knows."

Hey, Good Lookin'

SPRING was Ted's favorite time of year. Bright flowers. Sunny days. And now that the ice on the pond was gone, he could sit and admire his reflection again.

But this spring, Ted groaned the first time he saw his face in the pond. He counted two new wrinkles. Along with his old one, that made three.

"Peach pits!" said Ted. "I'm losing my looks."

When Janet jogged by, he called out, "Help! I'm getting old. What's your secret? *Your* skin is always so smooth and pink."

"It's true that nature's been extra good to me." Janet patted her cheek. "But eating slops and taking mud baths help a bit, too. Slops fill out the wrinkles. Mud tightens up the rest. And scrubbing it off gives a rosy glow."

Ted joined her for a mud bath that very afternoon.
The mud tightened up every feather he had. By the time
they'd scrubbed it off, Ted looked like he'd run backwards
through the holly hedge. The only glow he felt was a
burning in his stomach from the slops he ate, and he
still had all three wrinkles left.

"Why me?" Ted began to weep. "My good looks have *always* been my lucky charm."

"Relax," said Stella. "Getting sheared once a year keeps *me* looking young. You just need to get plucked. Worrying will only make your five wrinkles worse."

"FIVE!" screamed Ted. He ran to the pond to check his face again. Stella shook her head. "Poor Ted."

"I know," said Janet. "We've got to do something to cheer him up."

Three hours later, they'd hatched a plan. They found Ted sitting in the shade of the old pine tree.

"Good news!" said Stella. "We have an idea how you can keep your looks."

"That's sweet," said Ted. "But I haven't worried about *that* since I talked with Pearl."

Janet gave a humph. "What does *she* know?"

"Pine cones."

Stella laughed.

Janet gave a snort. "How in the world does putting pine cones on your face help anything?"

"Not my face." Ted smiled. "Tied to the bottom of my feet. It hurts so much to walk, I haven't thought of anything else since I put them on!"

Stella stared at Ted's feet. "They really work?"

"Like a dream," said Ted. "All your worries disappear in a flash."

"Sign me up!" said Stella.

"Me, too," Janet cheered.

"Just follow me." Ted slowly stood and began to hobble home. "I've—*Ouch*—got some—*Aiiee*—extra—*Yeow*—pine cones that—*Ouch*—you can use."

From that day on, Ted never ever worried about losing his looks. Though he did fret a bit about what color ribbon looked best with pine cones.

And life at Wise Acres went on with a smile. Friends all around. A song in the air. And such amazing good luck—the moon always came out just when they needed the light at night.